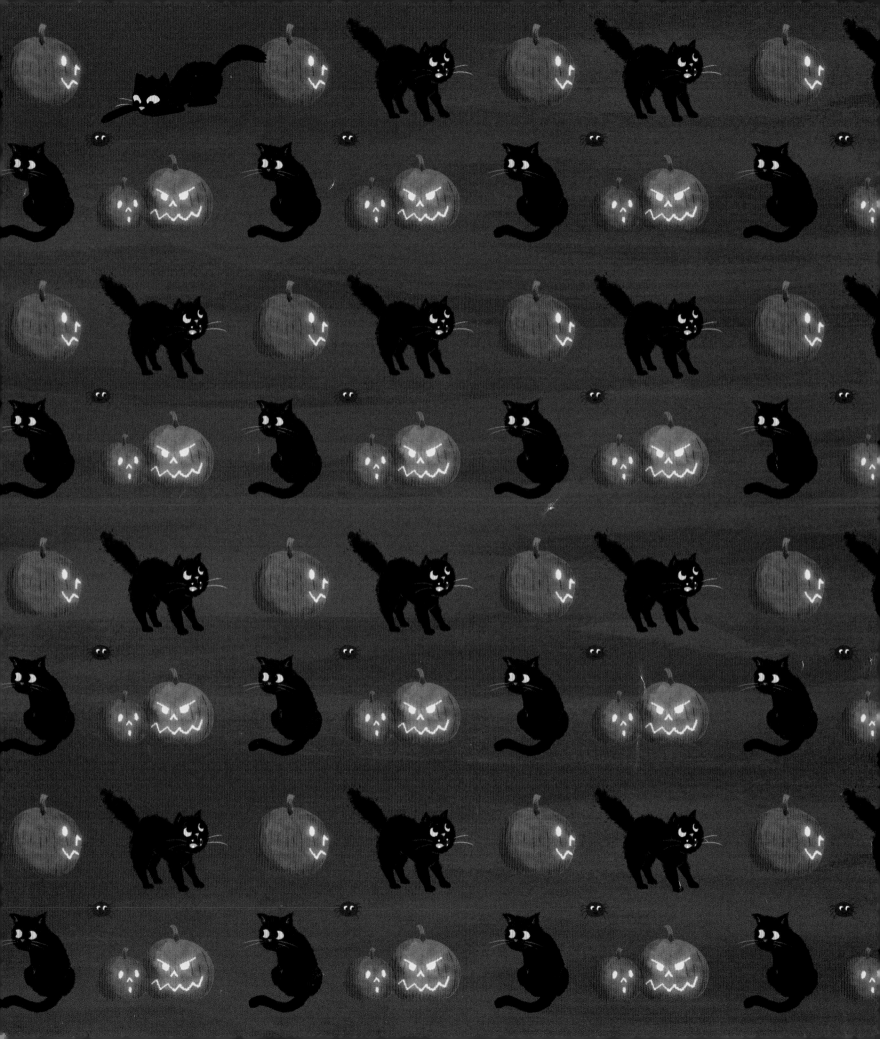

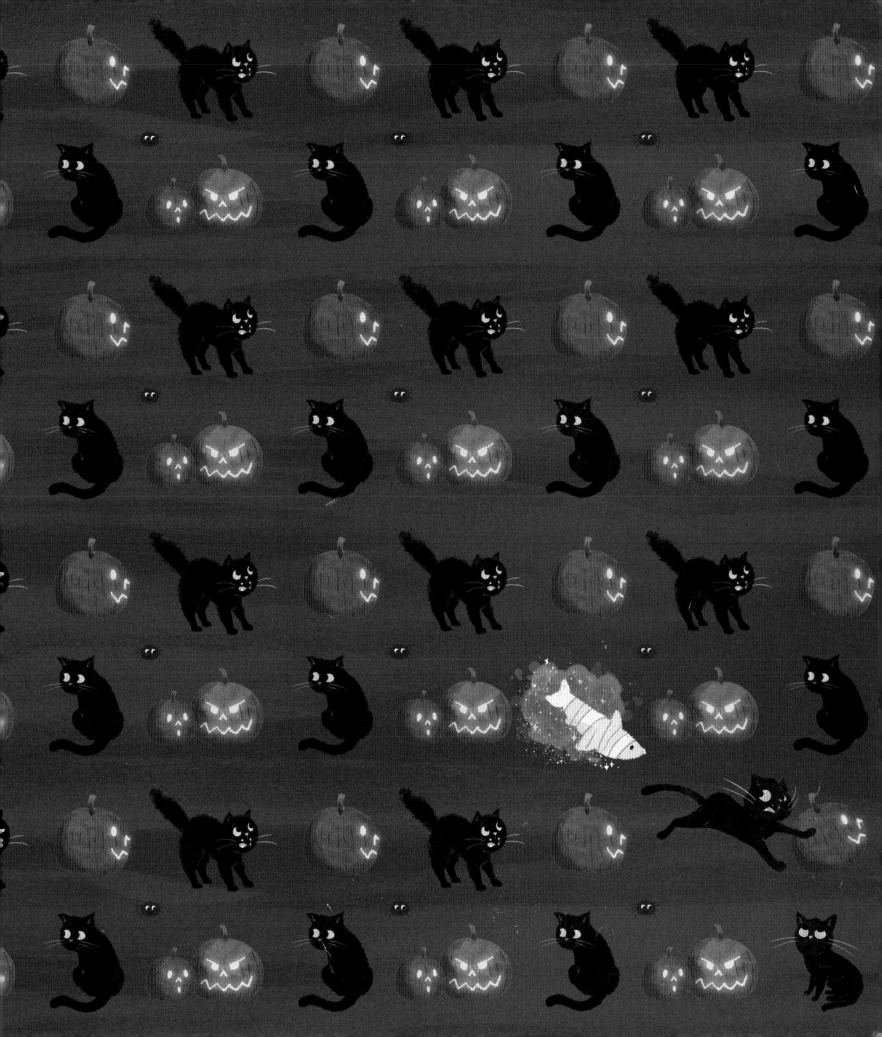

THERE'S A TROLL ON

For Harvey, Isla, Rosa and Frankie,
who all love Halloween
CJ

For my own two monsters,
Oscar and Harry
MB

First published in 2019 by Scholastic Children's Books
Euston House, 24 Eversholt Street, London NW1 1DB
a division of Scholastic Ltd
www.scholastic.co.uk
London ~ New York ~ Toronto ~ Sydney ~ Auckland ~ Mexico City ~ New Delhi ~ Hong Kong

Text copyright © 2019 Catherine Jacob · Illustrations copyright © 2019 Mike Byrne

PB ISBN 978 1407 18765 5 · C&F PB ISBN 978 1407 19244 4

MY TOILET

Catherine Jacob

Mike Byrne

■ SCHOLASTIC

There's a witch in my kitchen! She's boiling a brew,
mixing slimy green frogs' legs with pink gloopy goo.
She's stirring her cauldron and casting a spell.
Get out of here quick or she'll add you as well.

ABRACADABRA.
ABRACADEE.

Who else might we find here?
Come on, let's go see . . .

There's a skeleton
dancing a jig in my den!

She leaps through the air,

then

she

twirls

back

again.

The judges look **happy**.
In fact they're in **awe**.

They're up
on their feet.
She's done it.
Top score!

ABRACADABRA.
ABRACADEE.

Who else might we find here?
Come on, let's go see . . .

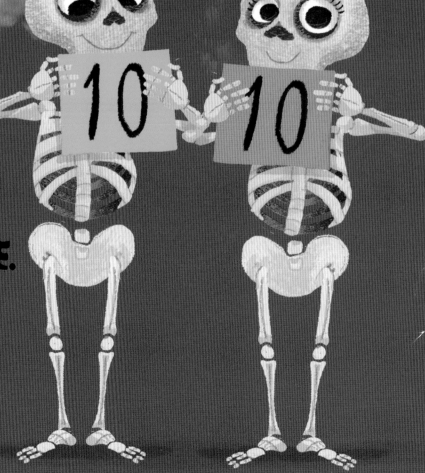

There's a troll on my toilet! He's blocked up the loo,
creating a stink with a huge troll-sized poo.
I'm holding my nose as he yanks at the chain.
Oh no! Call the plumber! He's blocked up the drain.

ABRACADABRA.
ABRACADEE.
Who else might we find here? Come on, let's go see . . .

There's a mummy magician upstairs in my room!
She's bandaging up lots of things for her tomb.

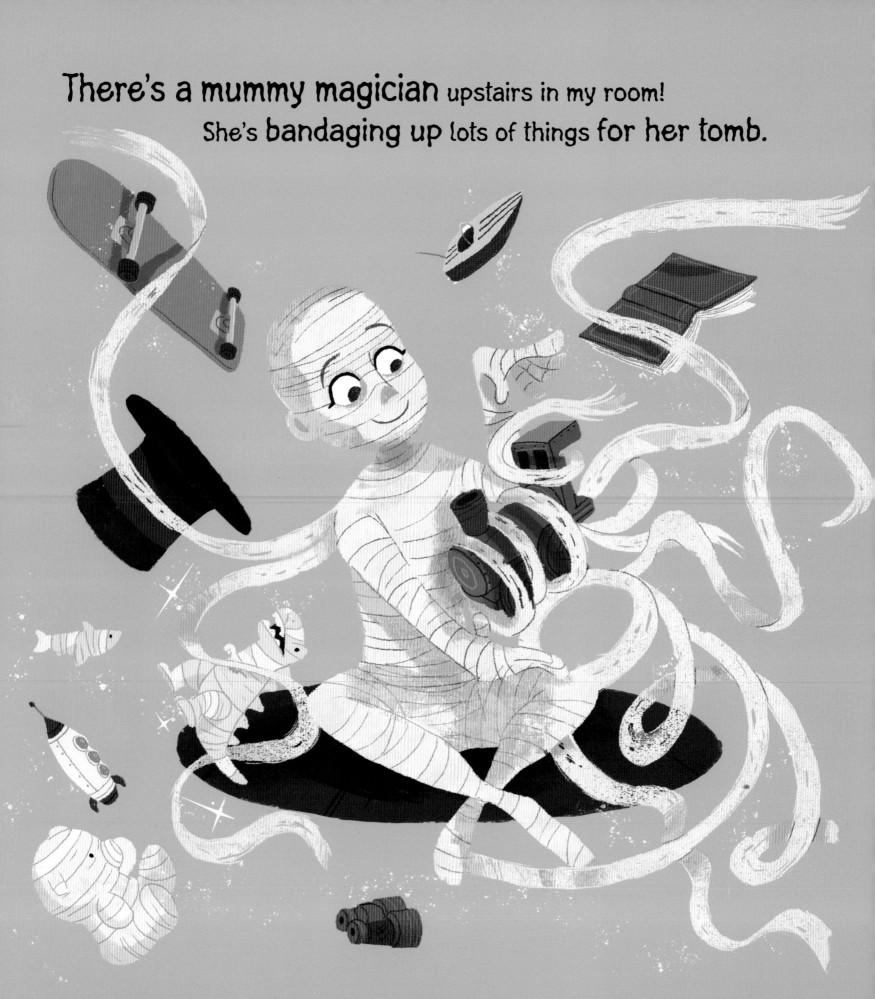

She **taps** her top hat
and cries,

"ALLA**KAZAT**!"

and lo and behold,
out jumps Mary our cat!

ABRACADABRA.
ABRACADEE.
Who else might we find here? Come on, let's go see . . .

There's a monster who's munching his lunch in my snug.
He snacks on worm sarnies and hot roasted slug.
Next course: bogey soup,
which he drinks with a SLURP!
Then slaps his full belly and does a big

BURP!

ABRACADABRA.

ABRACADEE.

Who else might we find here?
Come on, let's go see . . .

ZOMBIE
FLAKES

There's a **werewolf** who's **shrieking** away in my **shower!**
He **howls** at the **moon** – he's been in there an **hour!**

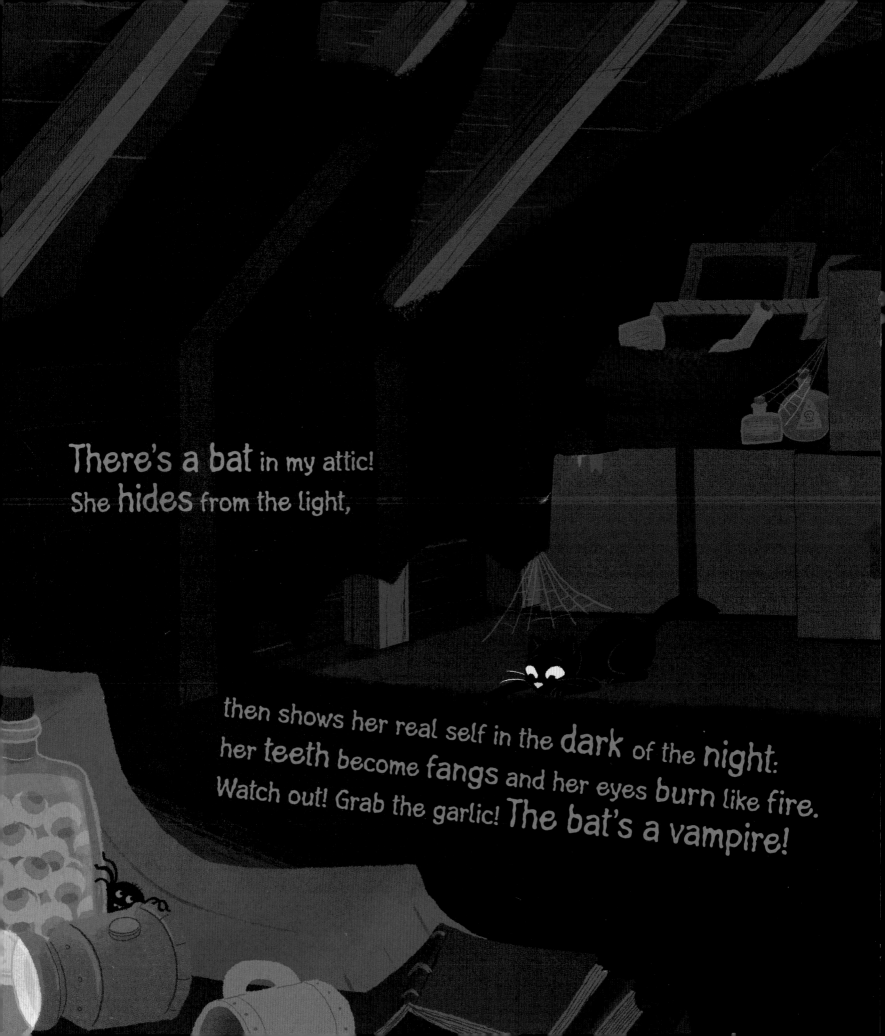

There's a bat in my attic!
She hides from the light,

then shows her real self in the dark of the night:
her teeth become fangs and her eyes burn like fire.
Watch out! Grab the garlic! The bat's a vampire!

There's a ghost on my staircase!
In fact there are three.
They're sliding downstairs on the bannister,

"WHEEE!"

They fly off the end and land BUMP! on the floor.

(Tomorrow their bottoms are going to be sore.)

ABRACADABRA.
ABRACADEE.
Who else might we find here? Come on, let's go see . . .

There's a zombie band
playing in my music room!
They're noisily **banging** the drums,

Bada **BOOM!**

They **PLONK** the piano
and **TWANG** the guitar.
One's down on his knees,
he's a **zombie** rock star!

So, is my house haunted? Did you get a fright?
Such strange goings-on in the dark of the night.
Who are all these monsters and ghouls that we've seen?

What's that? Yes, you've got it...

IT IS HALLOWEEN!

witch is my mum
the **ghost** is my brother.

The **wolf**
is my dad

and the **bat's**
my grandmother.

The **troll** is my grandpa,
the **mummy's** my sis.
The **monster's** her boyfriend.
(I hope they don't kiss!)

We're having a **party**, we're in **fancy dress**.
But which **one am I**? Now let's see, can you guess?
I'm here in this picture. I'll give you a clue:
I'm small, round and orange, **yes**, there I am . . .

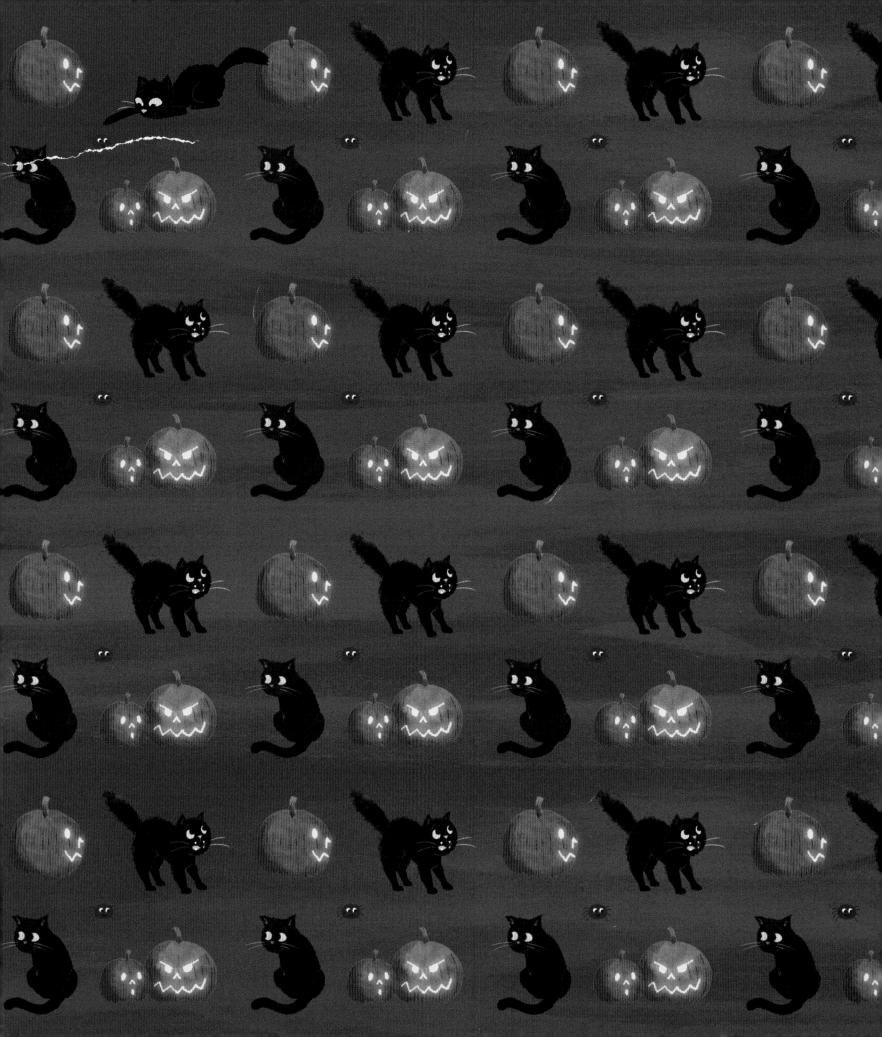

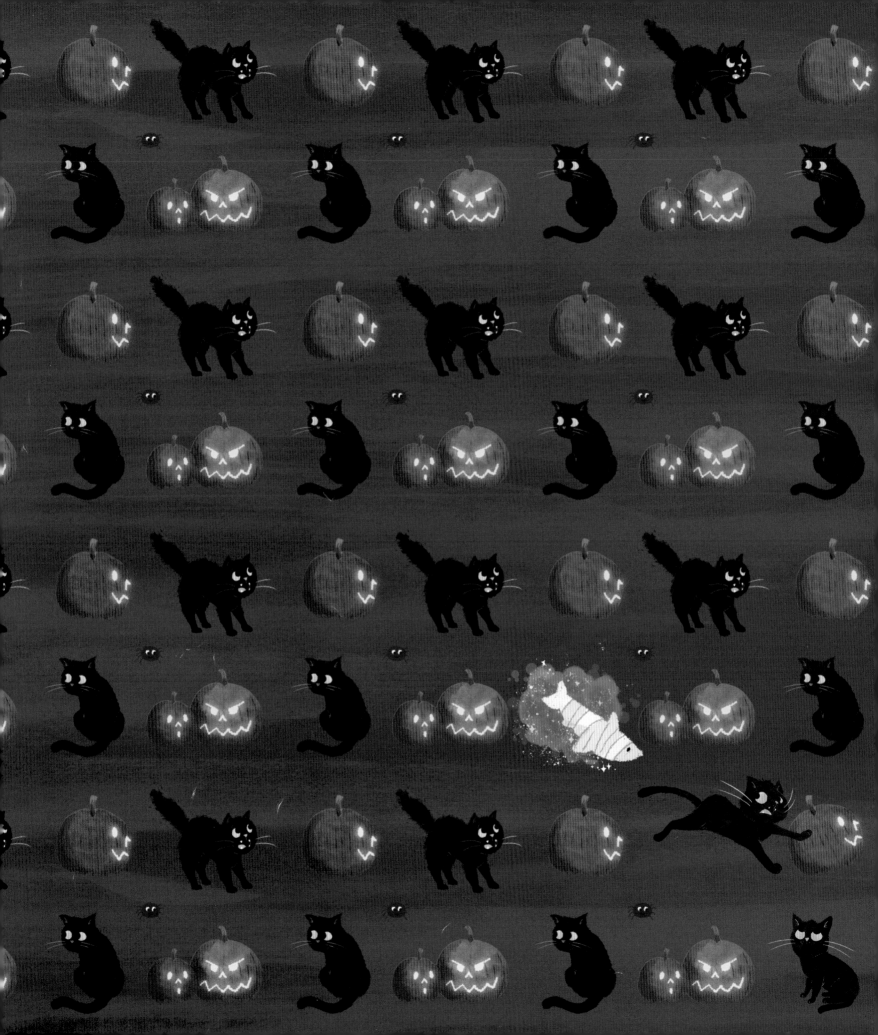